Fat Chance,

Story by Joan Lowery Nixon
Pictures by Tracey Campbell Pearson

VIKING KESTREL

VIKING KESTREL

Viking Penguin Inc., 40 West 23rd Street, New York, New York 10010, U.S.A.
Penguin Books Ltd, 27 Wrights Lane, London W8 5TZ (Publishing & Editorial) and
Harmondsworth, Middlesex, England (Distribution & Warehouse)
Penguin Books Australia Ltd, Ringwood, Victoria, Australia
Penguin Books Canada Limited, 2801 John Street, Markham, Ontario, Canada L3R 1B4
Penguin Books (N.Z.) Ltd, 182–190 Wairau Road, Auckland 10, New Zealand

Text copyright © Joan Lowery Nixon, 1987
Illustrations copyright © Tracey Campbell Pearson, 1987
All rights reserved

First published in 1987 by Viking Penguin Inc.
Published simultaneously in Canada

Printed in Hong Kong by Imago Publishing Ltd.
Set in Cheltenham Book

1   2   3   4   5   91   90   89   88   87
Library of Congress Cataloging in Publication Data
Nixon, Joan Lowery.   Fat chance, Claude!
Summary: A zany Texas couple, Shirley and Claude,
grow up and meet out in the gold mining hills of Colorado.
[1. Gold mines and mining—Fiction.   2. Colorado—
Fiction.   3. Humorous stories]   I. Pearson, Tracey
Campbell, ill.   II. Title.
PZ7.N65Fat   1987   [E]   87-8287   ISBN 0-670-81459-8

With love to
Nicholas Lowery Nixon
J.L.N.

CHAPTER ONE

In the little farming town of Hideyhole, nestled in the brown hills close to the edge of where the West begins, lived Henry and Maud and their daughter, Shirley.

Shirley was born long and lean, with hair the color of prairie dust and a mouth wide enough to hold a couple of smiles at the same time.

The Widder Swoose, who grannied all the babies in those parts, patted Shirley's fuzzy little newborn head and said, "Humph! So she's no beauty. Don't matter, 'cause I can tell right now Shirley's special, and she's not gonna be just like everyone else."

It wasn't more than half a dozen summers and snows before everyone found out that the Widder Swoose was right.

While other little girls were learning how to darn socks, Shirley was out in the fields learning how to rope a steer. While other little girls were baking ginger cookies, Shirley was breaking in a skittish colt. And while other little girls at school made flirty eyes at the boys in the next row, Shirley was actually listening to what the schoolmarm had to say.

But finally there came a time, years after Shirley had graduated from school, when Maud and Henry sat down in the front parlor with their daughter to have a serious talk.

"Shirley," her mama said, "every girl in town has got married, 'cept one."

"Who's that?" Shirley asked.

"You," her daddy said. "And it may have slipped your recollection, but those girls picked off all the unmarried men in town 'cept one."

"Yep," Shirley said. "Dull old Elmer Twaddle."

"That's no way to talk about a nice feller who's comin' callin' on you this evenin' with serious intentions," Henry said.

Shirley argued, and her daddy argued, and her mama burst into tears. "I don't want you to be an old maid!" Maud cried.

Shirley liked the idea of being an old maid, but she couldn't stand to see her mama all blubbery, so she gave in and said she'd at least sit on the porch swing with Elmer and hear what he had to say.

That evening, a few minutes before Elmer was due to come calling, Shirley put on her best store-bought dress and tied a red ribbon in her hair to match. Then she looked out her bedroom window and saw that someone had left the gate open to the back pasture and the bull was getting into her mama's vegetable patch.

Well, Shirley raced outside quicker than a horny toad off a hot rock. She yelled and waved her arms at the bull; but instead of trotting back to the pasture, that bull took one look at Shirley's red dress, put down his ugly head, snorted, pawed, and charged!

Shirley jumped on his shoulders, hanging on tight as he raced around the house, twisting and jumping and bellowing.

Finally the bull gave a mighty heave, and Shirley flew through the air and over the front porch railing. She sat up, brushed the hair out of her eyes, and looked up to see her mama, her daddy, and Elmer Twaddle.

"Howdy, Elmer," Shirley said, and she spit out a back molar that had been knocked loose.

"Excuse me," Elmer said, "but I just remembered someone I'm supposed to meet right now in another town." He jumped over what was left of the porch railing, climbed on his horse, and galloped off.

Maud began to cry.

Shirley got up, dusted herself off, and said, "It makes me no never mind, Mama. I don't want to get married. I've been hankerin' to go to Colorado and pan for gold."

Her mama wiped her eyes and blew her nose. "But I want to see my daughter as a happy bride."

Henry shook his head and patted his wife's shoulder. "Fat chance, Maud," he said.

CHAPTER TWO

Claude supposed he'd been a baby once. He didn't remember, and someone had penciled in a curly beard on the only baby picture of him that his mama had taken. Claude, who was as short as he was broad, worked hard on the family farm near the town of Flatplains, smack on the edge of where the West begins, taking care of his mama and his two younger brothers.

His brothers weren't much for farming. One day one of them said, "I want to be a doctor when I grow up." And the other said, "And I want to be a judge."

Claude said, "That'll take a heap of schoolin'." So he worked twice as hard and sent one brother to Harvard and the other brother to Yale. A few years after his brothers graduated, they got so rich they no longer needed to send their dirty laundry home to get it washed.

Then Claude's mama told him that she and the Widower Jones were going to get married.

"You'll like your six new brothers. They're smart as whips and eager for learnin'," his mama said.

"Mama, I wish you and the Widower Jones and all his sons well," Claude said. "But just this very minute I got a hankerin' to go West and look for gold."

So Claude got all the tools and provisions he needed and joined a wagon train heading for Colorado.

He swung his wagon into line behind a wagon with a long, skinny, friendly-smiling female driver. Shirley smiled at everyone. She was excited about looking for gold in Colorado.

That night they made camp near the river, with the moon making shadows and the coyotes howling like ghosts in the hills. After the mules had been cared for and the cookfires started, Shirley and Claude got acquainted.

"My mama sent along enough vittles to choke a cow," Shirley told Claude as she stirred the bubbling mixture in the stewpot. "You're welcome to share what I'm cookin' tonight."

Claude scowled and sat down on a rock. "It's plumb foolish for a woman to make this trip without a husband to take care of her," he said. "Why, you'll be as helpless as a burro in a blizzard if we run into trouble."

"No, I won't," Shirley said. "I got me a rifle and a quick wit, and I can't see what more I'd need."

"You ought to be home tendin' to a house," Claude said. "Instead, you're gonna be needin' this and needin' that and probably creatin' a terrible nuisance for all the menfolk on this train."

Well, while Claude was grumbling on, a mean, slimy, poisonous copperhead snake had slithered up from the river. Shirley spied it just as it slid onto the rock behind Claude. It raised its head, its beady eyes on Claude's back, its tongue flickering in and out as it waited to strike.

Shirley never was one to get into a head-on argument with a copperhead snake, so faster than a dragonfly on the way to becoming a fish's dinner she grabbed the handle of the stewpot and dumped the boiling stew on the copperhead, frizzling him so dead she totally changed whatever he had in mind.

Unfortunately, some of the hot stew got on Claude where he was sitting down, but as soon as he got through hopping around, Shirley pointed out the snake and explained what had happened.

Claude rubbed his backside. "I'm beholdin' to you for probably savin' my life," he said, "even though there mighta been a more comfortable way to do it."

"Glad to help," Shirley said.

"But take my advice, Shirley," Claude said. "Don't try to do somethin' a woman can't do. Go home, where you belong."

Shirley just smiled and looked down at Claude, eye to eye. "Fat chance, Claude," she said.

CHAPTER THREE

Since their wagons were together in line on the journey to Colorado, it was only fittin' for Shirley and Claude to become neighborly. Claude made beaten biscuits to go with whatever Shirley stirred together in the stewpot, and Shirley braced the broken spoke on Claude's wagon wheel with her best wooden stirring spoon.

Claude made flapjacks most mornings, and Shirley used the strings from a corset she wasn't planning to wear anyway to sew up a rip in the canvas on Claude's wagon.

Claude fed Shirley's mule when he fed his own, and when Claude came down with a cough and a case of the punies, Shirley gathered the right kind of herbs and tree bark and brewed him some tea that got him on his feet, feeling as frisky as a half-growed hound.

Finally they got to Colorado. Shirley said to Claude, "I'm gonna miss you, friend, but here's where I set off to look for gold."

"I wish you'd change your mind," Claude said. "I just don't know how you're gonna take care of yourself."

"Wish me luck," Shirley said.

So he did, and they parted company, both of them selling their wagons, packing their supplies on the backs of their mules, and setting out to look for gold in Cherry Creek.

For miles, men had staked claims and were working every inch of the creek. Shirley took her mule higher and higher, until finally she found a place at a sharp bend in the creek that nobody had claimed. It was lonely there. She thought about Claude and wondered how he was faring.

She pulled out her miner's pan and began to scoop the bottom, shaking out the pebbles, looking for the shiny yellow flecks that would mean gold.

On her third try she found a nugget the size of a horsefly. "Yahoo!" she shouted. "I'm gonna file me a claim!"

But a voice coming from around the bend in the creek said, "Not on my property, you ain't! I got here first, and I'm the one who's gonna file a claim."

Around the bend came Claude. "I shoulda knowed you'd show up, Shirley," he said. "You know this is gonna be my claim and my property, don't you?"

Shirley never was one to get into a head-on argument with a determined gold prospector, so she just smiled. "Fat chance, Claude," she said.

CHAPTER FOUR

It was too late in the day to head for the government office and file a claim. That night Shirley curled up in her bedroll and thought about Claude, whose loud snores were coming from the other side of the bend in the creek.

"What's more important, gold or friendship?" Shirley asked herself. She didn't have to think twice to come up with the answer.

In the morning she woke early and cleaned out her campsite. She went downcreek aways to freshen up and comb her hair and get ready to tell Claude that she was going to move on. But when she came back to the bend in the river, Claude had gone.

"Some friend!" Shirley shouted. She jumped on her mule and headed for town and the government claims office as fast as she could go. Claude had a head start, but maybe she could catch up.

When she finally burst through the door of the government office, she was hot and dusty, with her hair straggling in her face. There was Claude, near the end of the line.

"Shirley!" Claude shouted. "How come you took so long gettin' here, when you left afore I did?"

Everybody in the office turned to stare at Shirley. "I didn't leave afore you did!" Shirley shouted. "I was downstream, takin' a bath!"

Everyone looked at Claude.

"How'd I know that?" Claude said. "It ain't even Saturday."

"I was doin' some thinkin' last night," Shirley said.

"So was I," Claude said. "I was thinkin' that maybe we could be partners, Shirley."

"You mean work the claim together?" Shirley asked.

Claude pulled out a big handkerchief and wiped his face. He blinked and cleared his throat and stared down at his feet. Finally he said, "It ain't just the claim, Shirley. I got kinda used to you when we was on that wagon train, and I missed you when you was gone."

He didn't say anything else. "Go on. I'm listenin'," Shirley said, but Claude got sort of choked and didn't speak up.

"Go on. She's listenin'!" everybody in the office yelled at Claude.

He scowled at the floor and shouted, "A purty woman like you wouldn't want to marry an ugly old coot like me. You're gonna laugh in my face and turn me down."

Shirley never was one to get into a head-on argument with someone she loved. Her smile was so bright it lit up the office and all
the people who were standing there, grinning. She hugged Claude
so hard she lifted him right off his feet.

"Turn you down? Fat chance, Claude!" she said.